FOOTBALL FUGITIVE

FOOTBALL FUGITIVE

by Matt Christopher

Illustrated by Larry Johnson

Little, Brown and Company
Boston   Toronto   London

Library of Congress Cataloging-in-Publication Data

Christopher, Matthew F.
  Football fugitive.

  SUMMARY: Representing a pro football player whom his son admires brings a lawyer closer to his young son.
  [1. Football — Fiction. 2. Fathers and sons — Fiction] I. Johnson, Larry, 1949– II. Title.
PZ7.C458Fo   [Fic]   76–22778
ISBN 0-316-13971-8
ISBN 0-316-14064-3 (pbk)

HC: 10 9 8 7 6 5 4
PB: 10 9 8 7

VB

Published simultaneously in Canada
by Little, Brown & Company (Canada) Limited

PRINTED IN THE UNITED STATES OF AMERICA

To Christopher, Richard, and Nicole

DIGITS' ROSTER

Coach — Tom Ellis

OFFENSE

Curt Robinson	left end	88
Bobby Kolen	left tackle	74
Jim Collins	left guard	69
*Larry Shope	center	57
Greg Moore	right guard	26
Paul Scott	right tackle	70
†Ray Bridges	right end	32
George Daley	quarterback	7
‡Manny Anderson	left halfback	22
‡Billy James	right halfback	25
Doug Shaffer	fullback	72

DEFENSE

Rick Baron	left end	75
Steve Harvey	left tackle	71
Ed King	left guard	68
Charlie Nobles	right guard	66
§Joe Racino	right tackle	61
Chris Higgins	linebacker	52
Tony Foxx	linebacker	55
Jack O'Leary	defensive back	40
Pat DeWitt	defensive back; kicker	47

*Plays linebacker on defense.
†Plays right end also on defense.
‡Plays defensive back on defense.
§Substitutes as tackle and guard on offense.

1

GAME TIME WAS drawing nearer and nearer. And Larry Shope was getting more nervous by the minute.

He paced the room like a caged animal, glancing now and then out of the big plate-glass window. The sun was out and a breeze was blowing. You couldn't ask for better football weather.

"Larry," a voice said calmly, breaking into his thoughts.

He stopped pacing and looked at his mother, a tall, slim woman with black, shoulder-length hair. She was standing on the threshold of the door leading to the kitchen.

1

"You're going to wear a groove in that rug if you don't stop pacing back and forth like that," she said.

"What time is it?" he asked, fighting to control his nervousness.

She glanced at the clock in the kitchen. "Ten after four," she said, looking at him with a sunflower smile. "Don't you think you should be getting into your uniform?"

"Yeah," he said.

He went to his room and started to take off his clothes, his fingers trembling as he unlaced his shoes and unbuttoned his shirt. He wondered if his father would come home from his office in the city and offer him a word of cheer. *Good luck, son. Play hard and you'll come home a winner.*

Forget it. Dad was too busy with his very busy, very important law practice to think about him and *his* old football game.

He pulled on his pants, drew up the front laces, put on his shoulder pads. He was tightening the laces on them when he glanced at the picture in front of him. He paused and gazed straight at the eyes of the man in the picture.

They looked almost real. They were icy blue, set in a square-jawed face framed by sideburns that came about an inch below the ears. The man looked like a giant in his white, black-trimmed football uniform. "Bet his shoulders are five feet wide," Larry thought.

Across the lower right-hand corner of the picture was the inscription, *To Larry Shope, from Yancey Foote.*

"I guess that if I were as big as you, Yancey, I wouldn't have a thing to worry about," Larry said.

Six feet three, two hundred and forty-five pounds, thirty-one years old, Yancey had been a star player with the University of Southern California and is now a crushing guard with the Green Bay Packers. He likes to hunt and fish, and prefers being by himself to crowds. Larry knew Yancey's background like the back of his hand.

He finished dressing, sat on the bed and looked

at the picture again, then at the other pictures, all of Yancey Foote, which he had clipped out of newspapers and football magazines. Two walls were literally plastered with Yancey Foote pictures.

"I'm scared, Yancey," Larry whispered. "This is our first game and I'm scared to pieces."

He got up, went to the antiquated desk in the corner and pulled out the top drawer. A chill rippled through him as he looked at the letter at the top of the heap on the right-hand side. Stamped across the face of it were the words *Moved — Left No Forwarding Address.*

Larry picked it up. The one underneath it was stamped the same way. The third one was different. It was addressed to him in Yancey Foote's handwriting.

"I wonder where he's gone to," Larry thought. "He doesn't seem to be with the Packers anymore, but why hasn't he written to me telling me what happened? I don't understand it."

He laid the first letter aside, then took the letter out of the envelope addressed to him and unfolded it. The writing was in ink and neatly written, as if Yancey had taken a lot of pains over it.

Dear Larry,

Thanks for your recent letter. No, I don't think you're dumb for going out for football just because you're overweight. As a matter of fact, football should do you good. The important thing is to get in condition and learn the rules so you won't get hurt. Not that you will get real hurt, understand. Your kind of football isn't like the kind we pros play!

We lost a close one on Sunday. Did you watch it on television? Well, we have a tough opponent in the Vikings next Sunday, but we feel we can redeem ourselves.

Good luck.

> *Your pal,*
> *Yancey Foote*

That must have been the forty-ninth time he had read the letter. It gave him as big a lift now as it had done the first time he read it.

But that was Yancey's last letter to him. What had happened to him, anyway? Where had he gone to?

Larry put the letter away, pushed in the drawer and went to the kitchen, glancing at the door of his father's den which he sometimes used as an office. There was another door from the hall through which clients went to see his father, providing him with the privacy he needed for his law business.

"You sure you don't want a sandwich before you leave?" his mother asked him. "You're going to be pretty hungry by the time you get back home."

"That's okay. I'm not hungry," he said. That's because butterflies were flying around in his stomach.

He looked out the window. A kid in a black uniform with white stripes down the sides, just like the one Larry was wearing, was coming down the street.

"Greg's coming, Ma," said Larry. "I'll go now."

"Good luck," she said.

6

He went to the door, then turned and glanced back at her.

"Yes, Larry?" his mother asked.

Didn't Dad say he'd like to come to the game? he wanted to ask her. But he didn't.

"Nothing, Ma," he said, and went out.

2

"HI YA, GREG," said Larry, looking directly at him so that Greg could read his lips. "How do you feel?"

Greg shrugged his wide shoulders. He played right guard with the Digits, doing well in spite of his handicap; he was almost totally deaf.

"Shaky," he said.

"Why? You did all right in practice."

"I know," Greg replied in a low, awkward drawl. "But I'm still shaky!"

He laughed, and Larry laughed with him.

Greg had been deaf since birth, yet no one had ever doubted that he would make the team.

8

He attended a special school where he had learned to talk. Not being completely deaf, he was able to hear quarterback's signals if they were shouted loudly enough, and he was a fine player.

They arrived at the field, started to throw warm-up passes, then lined up for brief warm-up runs. Larry found that running and throwing relieved the tension that had built up inside him. He was ready to go.

The captains of both teams, Doug Shaffer for the Digits and Morris Hanes for the Whips, met at the center of the field with the referees. One of the refs flipped a coin.

"Heads!" said Doug, just loud enough to be heard from the bench.

He must have lost, because the ref put his hand on the other captain's shoulder, and made a receiving motion. Then he touched Doug's shoulder and made a kicking motion toward the north goal.

"Okay, defense," said Coach Tom Ellis, a former college player. "Get out there and reverse the situation. Okay?"

9

A thunder of applause greeted both teams as they ran out on the field. A ref tossed a football to Pat DeWitt, who placed the ball in position on the forty-yard line. Then both teams lined up for the kickoff.

Pat's toe met the ball slightly off center, sending it spinning like a top toward the left side of the field. It hit the ground in front of a Whips lineman, and bounced crazily until one of the running backs pounced on it.

The ref spotted it on the Whips' thirty-eight.

"Great start," grumbled Jack O'Leary, a defensive back.

"Maybe we're all a little nervous," said Larry.

"Why? What's there to be nervous about?"

Jack was tall and thin as a fence post. Larry remembered that Coach Ellis had quite a time finding shoulder pads that would fit him. Yet to hear him talk you'd think he didn't have an ounce of fear in him.

"Guess you're different," Larry said.

The Whips went into a huddle, broke out of it

11

and lined up at the scrimmage line. Larry settled in his middle linebacker position, his heart pounding. *One of the toughest positions on defense is the middle linebacker,* Yancey Foote had written in one of his letters. *You must be able to go in either direction, left or right.*

Mick Bartlett, the Whips' quarterback, barked signals. The ball was snapped. Mick backpedaled a few steps, then handed off to J. J. Jackson. Jackson plowed through the line where a hole had opened up wide enough to drive a truck through.

Larry's eyes met J. J.'s squarely as the fast-running back came toward him. Then, just as Larry reached out to grab him, J. J. made a lightning dodge to the left. Larry's fingers barely brushed against J. J.'s crimson shirt as J. J. burst by him, plunging to the forty-five, where Jack O'Leary pulled him down.

"Come on, you guys! Plug up that hole!" Jack yelled, straightening up his helmet and backing up to his position. Larry admired him. That was an excellent tackle.

12

Second and three.

J. J. carried again. This time he dashed through a hole on the right side of the line, picking up four yards and a first down before Rick Baron and Steve Harvey brought him down.

Pete Monroe, the Whips' burly fullback, tried to duplicate J. J.'s run up through the middle. The hole was there, but so was Larry. His feet planted squarely under him, Larry followed Pete's every move, determined not to be outfoxed this time.

Pete tried to stiff-arm him, dodging to his left in an attempt to evade Larry's reaching hands. He wasn't as quick as J. J., though, and Larry tackled him, pulling him down on the Digits' forty-eight. A three-yard gain.

Second and seven.

J. J. carried the ball again, sprinting around left end for a long gain and another first down. The Whips were moving, taking huge bites of precious yardage, and they seemed unstoppable.

In three more plays they hit pay dirt, J. J. going over for the touchdown. Then Pete swung around right end for the extra point. Whips 7, Digits 0.

Coach Ellis sent in his offensive team, keeping in Larry, Manny Anderson and Billy James, all of whom played defense and offense. Larry played center on offense; Coach Ellis had told him he had the size for both a center and a middle linebacker. Larry didn't know whether to be proud of that or not. Were he, Manny and Billy expected to play every minute of the game? With twelve minutes in a quarter that added up to forty-eight minutes. A guy could absorb a lot of beating in that time if he were lucky enough to live through it.

Omar Ross, the Whips' hefty middle linebacker, kicked off. The boot was a beauty, flying end over end deep into Digits territory. Doug Shaffer, the Digits' wing-footed fullback, caught it and ran it up to his thirty-three, where two Whips downed him.

"Eighteen," quarterback George Daley said in the huddle.

"Eighteen?" Doug echoed. "Man, you want to pass right off the bat?"

"They won't expect it," said George.

14

"But nobody ever starts off with a pass. Okay, you called it. Let's go."

"No. Wait a minute. Let's change it to twenty-eight."

Larry glanced from George to Doug. *Who's quarterbacking this team, anyway?* he wanted to ask.

"Right," said Doug. "Let's get 'em, guys."

They broke out of the huddle and hustled to the line of scrimmage. Larry felt an elbow nudge him on the arm. It was Greg. A questioning look was in his eyes. He hadn't heard what that exchange was about, but he could tell that it was not something pleasant.

Larry got over the ball, put his hands around it.

"Hut one! Hut two! Hut three!"

Larry snapped the ball, then threw a block on Omar as the linebacker tried to plunge through the line. Omar fell over him, regained his balance, and started after George. George backpedaled a few steps, turned and handed off to Billy James, the right halfback. Billy grabbed the ball and

15

sprinted toward the right side of the line. The Whips' defense went after him, caught him, and threw him for a three-yard loss.

"Maybe we should've tried the pass after all," Billy said in the huddle.

"You didn't get the blocking or you would've made it," said Doug defensively. "I don't care. Try a pass now if you want to."

George did. It was a long one, wobbling just slightly as it arched through the air, intended for wide receiver Curt Robinson. In every respect it was a beautiful pass, but George apparently had not accounted for J. J. Jackson. The spindle-legged backfield man seemed to come out of nowhere, plucking the ball out of Curt's hands and running with it down the field as if he were taking off with a pot of gold.

There was no stopping him as he sprinted down the sideline for a touchdown. It was a surprise blow. A sock in the gut.

"That guy's everywhere!" George said unbelievingly.

"You have to have your eyes peeled," said Doug, his own eyes glazed with fury at the sudden turnaround. "You just can't look at the receiver. Anyhow, Manny was wide open. You should've thrown to *him.*"

Larry's stomach twinged. "Don't blame George, Doug," he said. "He threw a good pass. J. J.'s so fast that I never saw him myself till he caught the ball."

"Why were you watching?" Doug shot back. "You were supposed to be blocking."

"I blocked my man," Larry answered, his anger mounting. "But I still had time to see if that pass was completed."

"Larry — no."

He felt a hand grab his arm. It was Greg's.

"Don't argue, Larry," Greg said. "It won't get us anywhere."

"Right," Larry thought. That Greg. He could not have heard a word of the exchange, yet he must have felt that Larry and Doug were having an argument.

18

Pete Monroe passed for the point after. It was good. Whips 14, Digits 0.

Three minutes into the second quarter the Digits made their first big gain, a thirty-six-yard run by Manny Anderson.

The ball was spotted on the Whips' twenty-six. First and ten.

"Forty-eight," said George in the huddle.

Forty-eight. Doug's carry around right end. George called signals, took the snap, handed it off to Doug. The fullback sped toward the right, eluded two would-be tacklers and was knocked out of bounds by the Whips' defensive backs. A three-yard gain.

"Forty-three," said George.

Doug carried it again, this time plunging through a hole in the line wide enough to let a trailer van through. Greg, left guard Jim Collins, Larry — they did their jobs skillfully and well. Larry went as far as throwing a block on another man besides his own, providing Doug the op-

19

portunity to gain an extra eight yards on top of the eleven he already had.

Then a flag dropped. A whistle shrilled. Larry stared at the ref as the man in the black-and-white striped shirt showed the clipping sign.

"On who?" asked Larry bewilderedly.

"On *you*," replied the referee grimly.

3

STUNNED, LARRY WATCHED the ref pace off fifteen yards against the Digits from the twenty-three, spotting the ball on the thirty-eight-yard line.

Third and twenty-two.

Clipping! What a stupid, inexcusable goof! You can't throw a block on an offensive guard from behind and not expect a penalty!

"Tough luck, Larry," Greg said, coming up beside him.

Larry pressed his lips hard together and shook his head.

"Sorry, guys," he said in the huddle. "I wasn't on the ball."

No one seemed to have heard him.

"Sixty-three flare pass," George said.

It didn't work. George's pass was far over the head of the intended receiver, left end Curt Robinson.

Fourth down. Pat DeWitt came in, replacing Doug. The team went into a punt formation. Pat kicked, a high, spiraling boot into the Whips' end zone.

The ball was brought back to the twenty. Whips' ball.

They moved it, J. J. Jackson doing most of the moving. His wide grin showed that he was enjoying it immensely.

"He's like grease," linebacker Chris Higgins said.

"Maybe he'll tire out after a while," said Tony Foxx, another linebacker.

"Sure," answered Chris. "After he scores another touchdown."

Yancey Foote came to Larry's mind. What would Yancey do in a situation like this? he asked himself. Let the Whips roll on? No. He'd go after the man with the ball, go after him with all the speed and power he had. He'd play above and beyond his normal capacities.

"I can try it," Larry thought. "That's the best I can do."

The signals. The snap from center. Mick Bartlett turned with the ball, waiting for J. J. to come and take it from him.

At the same time Larry, plunging past the center and the guard, exploded through the hole that his linemen had helped to create. A determined force drove him on, putting power and muscle into his legs and body that seemed not to have been there before. His rubber cleats chewed up the turf as he churned ahead, his head up, his eyes on his target.

He got to Mick a fraction of a second before J. J. did, throwing himself at the quarterback with outstretched hands, pinning Mick's arms in a viselike grip, knocking the ball loose, and then pouncing on it like a hungry cat on a field mouse.

Digits' ball!

They grabbed him, hugged him, jumped up and down with him.

"Nice play, Larry!" Greg cried. "Nice, nice, nice!"

They moved the ball to the Whips' eighteen when the four-minute warning sounded. Pat DeWitt's fourth down field goal from the eleven cracked the ice, but that was all for the first half. Whips 14, Digits 3.

Both teams retired to the school, the Whips to the gym, the Digits to the locker room.

"You guys really played your hearts out those last five minutes," said Coach Tom Ellis, smiling as he planted a foot on top of a bench. "Keep up that momentum in the second half and we should take 'em."

"That J. J. Jackson moves like a streak, Coach," Tony Foxx said. "I don't think he's human."

Coach Ellis laughed. "Was Larry Shope human when he busted through the line and forced Mick Bartlett to fumble the ball, then recovering it? It's that extra effort we have to use sometimes. Great play, Larry."

"Thanks, Coach," Larry answered, almost inaudibly. He liked the praise, but he couldn't forget his clipping penalty that had really hurt the team.

Maybe it was a good thing after all that his father didn't come to the game.

"Try some short passes, George," suggested the coach. "Just over the line of scrimmage. See what happens."

"Okay."

"Jack and Tony, I want you to concentrate on J. J., whether he runs or goes out as a receiver. Maybe double-teaming him will slow him down."

"I doubt it," said Tony pessimistically. "I think we ought to quadruple-team him, Coach. Bet he's already tied O. J. Simpson for rushing yards in one game."

Again the coach laughed. "No, you do as I say," he insisted, "and we'll see what happens. They're only eleven points ahead."

By the end of the third quarter the Whips were another touchdown ahead, the third one resulting from a long pass to J. J. Jackson in the end zone. Jack and Tony had been double-teaming him, but on that pass J. J. had outrun Jack, and might have — or might not have — outrun Tony. No one would ever know because Tony, running side by side with J. J., had slipped, lost his balance and fallen. J. J. had caught the ball, then raised it high over his head while he did his touchdown dance, pumping his legs up and down as if he were beating a drum with his feet.

This time the try for the extra point failed. Whips 20, Digits 3.

"I still think we ought to quadruple-team him," insisted Tony.

"Will you cut out that quadruple stuff?" Jack snorted. "Whoever heard of quadruple-teaming a guy, anyway?"

"That's putting four men on him, in case you didn't know," said Tony, glaring at Jack.

"Man, listen to the walking dictionary," replied Jack. "You know what? I think you should've intercepted that pass."

"I would have, but I slipped," said Tony, seriously. "I suppose you don't believe me."

"Yes, I believe you," Jack grunted, stamping off toward the line of scrimmage in a huff. "Anything to end this stupid argument."

"Hooray!" thought Larry, happy that the angry exchange ended, too. This was no time for intra-team squabbles.

With one minute gone of the fourth quarter, and the ball in the Digits' possession on their own forty-two, Coach Ellis sent in a play via Joe Racino, who took Bobby Kolen's place at left tackle.

"Forty-eight right pass," said Joe.

The play code started flashing in Larry's mind. Doug Shaffer and Ray Bridges were the pass receivers, Ray the main target. If he were too well covered, the pass was to go to Doug. If Doug was also covered, well — it was George's option what to do then. "The headaches of a quarter-back," thought Larry. "I don't envy him one bit."

27

They broke out of the huddle and went to the line of scrimmage. It was first and ten.

"Hut one! Hut two! Hut three!"

Larry snapped the ball, then barged forward, throwing a block on the middle linebacker's right side. But Omar Ross, after falling down from Larry's charge, got up again and exploded forward. He was nowhere near Ray, though, as the speedy right end bolted up the field some five yards ahead of two Whips defensemen.

For a moment Ray slowed down and waited for George's long, spiraling pass, which reached him before the defensemen did. He caught it, but the change of pace was just enough for one of the Whips to nail him before he advanced any farther.

First and ten, on the Whips' twelve.

Bobby came back in, as messenger for another play from the coach, and Joe ran out.

"Forty-two run," said Bobby.

Again the play code, calling for Doug to plunge through the two hole, flashed through Larry's mind.

"We're twelve yards from home," said George in the huddle. "Let's make it, man!"

They broke out of the huddle and trotted to the line of scrimmage. George barked signals. Larry snapped the ball, charged forward, threw a weak block on Omar. At the same time Greg rammed against his man, and for a moment there was plenty of daylight for Doug to run through.

But Omar pulled him down on the right side.

"He got away from Larry," panted Doug in the huddle. "I could've gone another three or four yards."

Larry fumed. Why was Doug picking on him? Everyone makes mistakes.

"Okay, let's try it again," said George. He made fists of his hands as he glanced at Greg, the sign that the same play was on. Greg acknowledged with a nod.

"Here we go again," thought Larry. "What am I supposed to do? Put a scissor hold on Omar so he can't break loose? He's as tough to block as J. J. is to tackle."

But he did block Omar, while Greg blocked his man, just long enough for Doug to plow through for five more yards and a first down.

First and goal.

"Want to try it again, Doug?" George asked, apparently assured of Doug's ability.

Doug, breathing hard, smiled. "Why not?" he said.

The signals. The snap. The plunge.

But the daylight wasn't there now. The Whips had formed an impenetrable wall at the scrimmage line, and Doug, striking it, had bounced back. It was a shattering blow to the Digits.

"How about a pass, George?" suggested Curt.

"Okay. In the corner," said George.

It worked. Doug kicked for the point after and it was good. Whips 20, Digits 10.

"Only a miracle," thought Larry, "could pull the Digits out of this one."

The miracle didn't happen. Neither team scored again, and the Digits walked off the field the loser.

"Somebody wins, somebody loses," said Omar, walking next to Larry and Greg.

"It's only a ball game," replied Larry, not looking at him.

As they reached the side of the bleachers, Greg nudged Larry on the arm.

"Larry, look!" he exclaimed. "You ever see a guy bigger than he in your life?"

Larry followed Greg's gaze to a man standing beside the bleachers. For a second his pace slowed down as the size of the man struck him. The man was wearing dark sunglasses and Larry's heart pounded as he felt the man's eyes focused directly on him.

The stranger was over six feet tall, had long sideburns, an inch-long beard, was broad-shouldered and wore a hat and a brown jacket.

Something in Larry's bones told him that he had seen the man somewhere before.

4

WHY WAS THE MAN watching them play? "Could it be he knew someone on the team?" wondered Larry. "If so, why was he staring at me?"

They reached the street and Greg asked, "Did you ever see him before?"

"Never," answered Larry.

He looked over his shoulder, wondering if the stranger might be walking behind them. Sure enough, he was. But he was by himself among all the uniformed players and spectators, a giant among Lilliputians.

Larry and Greg turned left on Catherine Street.

After a while they saw the crowd, including the stranger, continue up Elm Street. Just for a moment Larry hoped that the man would look in his direction, but the stranger kept looking straight ahead.

"I guess he wasn't really looking at me," thought Larry. A spark of hope — that someone had taken a keen interest in his playing — flickered and died.

He tried to push the thought of the stranger out of his mind, and forced a smile. "After a few plays I wasn't scared anymore. Were you, Greg?"

"Scared of what?"

"Oh. Getting banged up."

Greg laughed. "Not me. I loved it!"

The bright, happy smile on his face was additional proof that he had.

"Didn't you?" he asked.

Larry shrugged. "Oh, sure. I loved it, too."

He wasn't sure that he did, though. And he had lied a little when he said that he wasn't scared anymore.

He thought of something else.

"Why didn't your parents come to the game?" he asked.

Greg looked at him with raised eyebrows, and he had to repeat the question.

"Oh," said Greg. "Dad works out of town. It takes him an hour to get home."

"Does he like football? Is he interested in your playing?"

"Is he? He's crazy about it. I bet he'll ask me to tell him about the game before I even sit down to eat!"

"That's great," said Larry.

"Does your father like football?" Greg asked.

"Yes. He likes it," said Larry, looking straight ahead.

"What?"

"I said he likes it," said Larry, looking at Greg now. "He's crazy about it, too."

"Then why didn't he come to the game?"

"He's a lawyer," said Larry. "He works crazy hours. Some clients call him up even at night. I bet the minute I get inside he'll want to know all

34

about the game, too. That is, if he's not busy with a client."

"I guess your father must be a great guy, too, Larry," Greg said.

"Yeah, sure," Larry replied softly.

It wasn't like what Larry had said when he entered the house. The first thing Mom said was, "Don't come into the house with those dirty shoes. Take them off on the porch."

He took them off, left them on the porch and walked into the house in his dirty socks. He strode past his mother and headed for his bedroom.

"Get your clothes and change in the bathroom," she said.

Not "Who won the game? Did you play? How well did you play?" Just "Get your clothes and change in the bathroom."

He glanced into the living room before going up the stairs and saw his father sitting by the window, his legs stretched out and crossed at the ankles. He was asleep.

Larry thought about what he had told Greg

would happen the instant he entered the house, and felt a lump rise in his throat. Well, Dad couldn't sleep and ask him questions about the football game at the same time, could he?

He got his clean clothes out of the bedroom, stripped off his uniform, showered and dressed. As he came out and headed for the kitchen his father surprisingly called to him, "Well, who won?"

His heart thumped. "They did," he answered.

"Who's 'they'?"

"The Whips."

"What was the score?"

"Twenty to ten."

"Good game," said his father.

That's all he said as he rattled his newspaper and started to read.

"Come on," said Larry's mother. "Your dinner's ready."

Before going to bed that night he wrote a letter to Yancey Foote, hoping that this time Yancey would receive it.

Dear Yancey,

We played our first game today and lost, 20 to 10. It was a battle, although the Whips were ahead of us all the time.

I played center on offense and middle linebacker on defense, and Coach Ellis had me play most of the game. My best play was tackling the Whips' quarterback, forcing him to fumble the ball. Then I recovered it. The only thing that resulted from that play, though, was a field goal. Our only touchdown came in the fourth quarter.

I hope that you receive this letter, Yancey. I haven't heard from you lately, but I hope that isn't because you got tired of receiving letters from a kid. If that is the reason, I understand.

No matter what the reason is, though, I will always be

Your friend,
Larry

He read the letter over, addressed an envelope, put the letter into it and sealed it. He considered and reconsidered putting a stamp on it, then decided to wait till morning.

In the morning the question persisted: Why waste a stamp? If the last two letters came back why wouldn't this one come back also?

Nevertheless, he stuck a stamp on it and dropped it in a mailbox on his way to school. There was always hope. And what's a stamp?

During the course of the day Yancey Foote popped in and out of his mind like a Jack-in-the-box. It occurred to him that he might be able to find out about Yancey if he wrote to the Packers football team. Perhaps a letter to the coach would invite an answer and an explanation as to what happened to Yancey.

There was another possibility. A recent issue of a football magazine might have something about him. It might clear up the mystery of why the letters to him were returned.

The last period of the school day was the longest Larry had spent in weeks. He couldn't wait till the buzzer sounded. When it did he was among the first out of the room, not even waiting for Greg to accompany him home as he usually did. Right now nothing was more important than to get to a magazine store.

There was one on Palm Street. Dad stopped there every Sunday after church to pick up the *New York Times.* The store was several blocks out of the way, but — so what?

He arrived there, breathing hard from the long run from school, and started to look for the sports magazines. They were all on one shelf, practically at his eye level, magazines covering all the major sports: baseball, basketball, soccer, tennis, football.

He glanced over the featured titles of the football magazines. Familiar names stood out like neon lights: Joe Namath, O. J. Simpson, Larry Csonka, Ed Marinaro.

And then his heart jumped as he recognized another name, and read the long title: *Yancey Foote — Good Guy or Bad Guy?*

Good Guy or Bad Guy? What in the world did that mean?

His heart still jumping, Larry looked for the

price of the magazine. It was a dollar. Oh, man, a dollar. He would have to borrow it from his parents; he seldom had any savings.

He ran all the way home, borrowed a dollar from his mother, then got back to the store as quickly as he could and purchased the magazine. He couldn't wait to get home again to read the article about his friend, Yancey Foote.

5

THE ARTICLE STARTED off with a bang.

What happened to that big, bone-crushing guard of the Packers, Yancey Foote? Nobody seems to know.

Could it have something to do with his seriously injuring a citizen in a bar-room squabble? There's no question about the fact that Foote vanished after paying $5000 in bail.

Although the incident has been hushed up by all concerned, Yancey's victim still lies in the hospital. But why should

Yancey Foote, a former USC football star and runner-up for the Heisman Trophy, suddenly disappear? Is it because this tough Packer is afraid he might be found guilty when his trial comes up in the fall?

Friends of the big guy have begun to wonder about him: What is he — a good guy or a bad guy? Did he really start the fight, or did the other guy — a man some fifty pounds lighter than the vanished pro? Did the man step too hard on the toes of the football star whose close friends had always considered him an easy-going, mild-mannered guy?

Larry couldn't believe it. Was it really Yancey Foote he was reading about? Was he the kind of guy who would beat up a man fifty pounds lighter than himself?

There must have been a reason behind it. A darn good reason. Yancey wouldn't beat up anybody unless he was provoked.

But, as the article said, why should he suddenly disappear? Did he really believe he was guilty and was afraid to face the consequences?

There was more to the article, but Larry just skimmed over the rest of it. A full-page color picture of Yancey bulldozing through the line after the ball carrier was opposite the title page of the article. The picture was so clear that, with a little imagination, you could almost hear the grunts and the groans, and the pounding of cleated shoes on the turf.

There in the article was the answer as to why Larry's letters to Yancey had come back. It was plain that it wasn't any use to write to the Packers. Even they didn't know where Yancey was — unless it was a secret that they had refused to tell the writer of the article.

Larry closed the magazine and placed it on a shelf in his room. He tried to avoid looking at the pictures of Yancey hanging on the walls, but they attracted him like magnets.

"Where have you disappeared to, Yancey?" he

43

said aloud to one of the pictures in which Yancey was standing, hands on his hips and a grim look on his face.

With a heavy heart he left the room, intending not to return to it again until bedtime. He didn't want Yancey's pictures reminding him of that question posed by the title in the football magazine: *Yancey Foote — Good Guy or Bad Guy?*

The next day he told Greg Moore about the article. Although Greg had never written a letter to Yancey Foote, nor to any other football player, he sympathized with Larry.

"Maybe he's gone away on a vacation," he said. "The Caribbean, or someplace like that, where nobody knows him."

"But why would he want to do that?"

"To get away from reporters," replied Greg, who was an avid newspaper reader. "Once the story broke, a famous guy in his situation would be hounded by reporters all the time."

"Yeah, I guess you're right," Larry answered thoughtfully.

There was practice after school and Coach Ellis had Larry work out at center. Larry did okay centering the ball, but was poor at blocking. He couldn't seem to put his entire effort into it, getting tossed aside like a windblown leaf when, instead, he should have been doing the tossing.

"C'mon, c'mon, Larry," Coach Ellis laid into him. "You're daydreaming. Get with it."

Daydreaming was right; thinking constantly about Yancey Foote's plight was what was causing Larry to perform so poorly.

The Digits had been practicing for nearly half an hour when Greg suddenly tapped Larry on the arm and said, "Larry, look who's standing there by the bleachers."

Larry looked, and saw the big man with the sunglasses and short beard. The same man who was at the Whips game last Wednesday.

All at once he felt a cold sensation sweep through him. He felt glued to the spot, his eyes riveted on the man, while a thought raced through his mind like wildfire.

It can't be, he told himself. Yet — why not? Why can't that man be Yancey Foote? The magazine article said that nobody knew where he was, didn't it? Well, why couldn't he be here in Glen Rose, a town where hardly anyone would know him?

Just then the man lifted a hand, and his face broke into a smile. Larry, surprised, looked around, but saw no one else except Greg looking at the man.

"It's us he must be waving and smiling at!" Larry thought.

Hesitant at first, he then quickly jerked up his hand and waved back. He saw the man nod, saw the smile broaden just a little.

"He's waving to *you*, Larry," said Greg softly. "How about that?"

"Larry! Greg!" Coach Ellis boomed. "If you guys are too tired to play maybe you'd like to sit this one out!"

"Sorry, Coach," said Larry, and socked Greg lightly on the shoulder. "C'mon, Greg. Let's get with it."

They worked on pass plays and line plunges, Larry centering the ball for the offensive team. Then the coach switched the squads, putting Larry in the middle linebacker position with the first team.

Larry couldn't get the image of the guy in the brown jacket out of his mind. He was ninety-nine percent sure it was Yancey Foote, yet why would Yancey be watching *him* play? His concern was reflected in his workout. And Coach Tom Ellis noticed it.

"Larry! You got lead in your feet? George got the ball and had faded back five yards before you had even *budged!*"

And another time, "Larry! On a line buck you charge in *after* the ball carrier, not wait for him to come to you!"

"Sorry, Coach," Larry said, embarrassed in front of all the guys.

He heard Doug's familiar, mocking chuckle. Somebody else picked it up, but a verbal blast from the coach ended it instantly.

"Cut it out, you guys, and get back on the line!"

47

he ordered firmly. "Let's go through that play again! On three!"

As the men hustled to the line of scrimmage, Larry glanced again toward the bleachers. But the man in the brown jacket was gone.

6

THE HELMETS OF the Moon City football
team were royal blue, with a picture of the moon
on them. Their blue satin, red-striped uniforms
looked fresh out of a laundromat.

It was Tuesday, October 7, and the Digits'
second game of the season. The sky was an ashen
gray, with a golden circle in the spot where the
sun was trying to shine through. It never made it.

"Twenty-one! Twenty-four! Hike! Hike!"

Larry, playing middle linebacker, a couple of
yards behind Charlie Nobles and Joe Racino,
plunged to the right the moment he saw Walt

49

Fregoni, Moon City's quarterback, hand off to his fullback, Bruce Green. Bruce hugged the leather against him like a loaf of bread and came bolting through the left side of his line. A hole opened up only wide enough to slip a piece of cardboard through, but Bruce came on like a flying wedge, his knees pumping high, his rubber cleats clawing the dirt.

Fear flashed through Larry and was gone almost as quickly as it had come. It was gone because Bruce was upon him before Larry could think about it.

He wrapped his arms around Bruce and felt the impact of Bruce's body at the same time. Down he went, his head smacking against the ground, Bruce on top of him, for a four-yard gain.

Bruce pressed against Larry's shoulders as he lifted himself to his feet. He was a tall kid and no lightweight. His dark eyes bored through the mask of his helmet into Larry's, but his face was as blank as a plastic doll's.

He carried the ball again, this time making a

wide sweep around his left end. Rick Baron was thrown a block; Billy James lost his footing and fell. It was up to Larry or the safety man to bring him down — or Bruce would go for a touchdown.

Larry, legs pumping like pistons, reached Bruce, got hold of his right arm and went down to his knees. Bruce stopped, spun around, freed himself from Larry's hold and plunged ahead for eight more yards before Jack O'Leary grounded him.

The run gave Moon City a first down.

Jack got to his feet, giving Larry a cold, shriveling look.

On the next play Walt handed off to Alan Stevens, his left halfback. Alan fumbled the ball, but recovered it just before Digits men got to it. It was a four-yard loss.

Second down and fourteen.

Walt tried a pass. That didn't work, either. Bruce carried again and gained six yards, but it was now fourth and eight.

They had to punt.

The ball spiraled into the sky, then rolled into the end zone and was brought out to the twenty.

The Digits' offense came in. It wasn't a complete change, mostly the line and two of the backs. Manny Anderson took the handoff on the first play and went for two yards. Then Doug collected eleven for a first down.

He was given another chance, but this time Moon City held him to two yards. Then George faded back to pass. Right end Ray Bridges ran down the field like a cat, then stopped short and waited for the ball to come to him.

It never did. George's pass, a beautiful spiral with hardly a wobble, was taken out of Ray's hands by a Moon City back, who galloped down the sideline with not a single Digit getting near him.

Touchdown.

The kick for point after was good. 7–0, Moon City.

"You ever notice how quick a situation can change?" Greg said to Larry as they walked across the field.

"Do I ever. That's the second time an interception's been run back for a TD," said Larry.

He thought of the man in the brown jacket again, but was too embarrassed to look toward the bleachers to see if he was there. Maybe Larry wasn't as embarrassed as George, who had thrown that errant pass. But he was embarrassed nevertheless. The team was an eleven-man unit. When a blow like that happened — no matter who was at fault — every man felt it.

Just before the teams got into position for the kickoff, Larry, his embarrassment forgotten, glanced toward the sideline. A crowd was lined up behind the rope that was strung along the full length of the field. The bleachers were filled, but there was no mistaking the tall figure in the brown jacket. He was there, towering like a giant statue, his arms crossed, his sunglasses like the black holes of a skull.

"Wonder what he thinks of us after that play?" Larry thought.

The Digits took the kickoff and went thirty-five

yards before they were forced to give the ball up to Moon City. Moon City kept threatening to score again, but it wasn't until the second quarter when they finally pulled it off.

It was Moon City 14, Digits 0 when the first half ended.

"He's here," Larry said as the team headed for the locker room.

"Who? The big guy?" asked Greg.

Larry nodded. "I wonder who he is? I have a suspicion, but I'm not sure."

"You have a *suspicion?* You mean you think you *know* him?"

Greg stared at Larry's lips as if he weren't sure he had read them right.

Larry met Greg's eyes squarely. "I said that I'm not sure, Greg. I just have a suspicion."

"That's what I thought you said," replied Greg. "Okay, are you going to tell me who you think he is, or do I have to guess?"

Larry hesitated before answering. He could

trust Greg to keep a secret, but what if his suspicion were wrong? Even Greg would laugh at him then.

"I've got an idea," Greg spoke up. "Let's follow him home after the game."

Larry looked at him. "Why?"

Greg lifted his shoulders. "See where he lives."

"What difference would that make?"

"Well, as least we'll find out where he lives."

"Okay. We'll do that," agreed Larry.

The talk that Coach Ellis gave the boys in the locker room was an attention-grabber. He had a knack of telling a kid about his mistakes so that the kid would never forget it. As for the kid committing the same mistake again, though, there was no guarantee. That depended on the kid.

The coach picked on them all. Some he spent ten seconds on, some sixty. You would think that all he had been doing was just watching the poor part of each player's performance, so that he'd have something to say during the intermission.

"Did you get all that?" Larry asked Greg as they left the locker room to start the second half.

"I think so. I'm not sure. Most of the time the coach doesn't open his mouth very much when he speaks, except when he sees me frowning at him. Every time I frown he knows that I'm not reading his lips very well, so he starts talking a little louder and forms the words with his lips. Didn't you notice that?"

"Yes, I noticed," Larry replied. "But how do you know he raises his voice?"

Greg shrugged. "I can tell. And, remember, I'm not totally deaf, either."

If Coach Ellis's halftime game analysis was an inspiration to his team, the coach of Moon City must have been equally inspiring. All the Digits managed to score was one touchdown, and that on a fluke sixty-four-yard run by Doug Shaffer after he had recovered a Moon City fumble.

When he scored, he jumped four feet into the air and tossed the ball up another twenty or so.

He also kicked the extra point successfully.

Moon City passed for a touchdown before the third quarter was over, then repeated the feat in the fourth. Neither time did Bruce Green succeed in booting the ball between the uprights for the point-afters, but it turned out that they were not needed, anyway. Moon City copped the game, 26 to 7.

"Are we going to follow the man?" Larry said to Greg as the teams walked off the field.

"We said we were," Greg replied.

Following the big man in the brown jacket was about as easy as following a white line. The boys remained slightly more than half a block behind him. Spectators and players of both teams filled the space in between.

After each block the number of spectators and players diminished as some of them turned off to go to their homes. By the time Larry and Greg had reached the fifth block there were just a handful separating them and the man.

"I wonder how far he's going," said Larry.

"Not too far, I hope," said Greg. "My parents will start worrying about me."

At the next block the man turned left.

"Hey, we don't want to miss him," cried Larry, and started running. Greg followed suit.

They reached the corner, turned it, and stopped as if they had run into a brick wall.

There he was, some twenty feet away, facing them with a smile that showed milk-white teeth.

"Hi, guys," he said pleasantly. "Sorry you lost the ball game. But that's how the cookie crumbles, isn't it?"

7

LARRY'S FACE turned scarlet. He felt like a fool, and wished he could make himself disappear.

But he couldn't. He just had to stand there — as Greg was standing there — and be embarrassed.

The man looked a lot like Yancey Foote. Yet those glasses and that beard made him look different.

"Okay, now. Relax," said the man. "I noticed you following me about two blocks away. Any reason why?"

The boys looked at each other. "How can I answer him?" Larry thought. "How can I tell him that I think he's Yancey Foote if I'm not absolutely sure he is? He'd laugh at me."

"We're sorry," Larry said. "We — we have no reason."

The man smiled. "Can I buy you a Coke, or a cone of ice cream? After a tough game you must have worked yourself up for a treat."

"No, thanks," Larry said. "We'd better go home."

"Okay. Take care now."

"Yes, sir. And — so long, sir."

Larry and Greg turned and left as if they were functioning on one brain.

"What a couple of stupes we are," Larry said disgustedly. "We should've known — well, me, anyway — that he might have spotted us following him."

"Well, we were real close to him before he turned the corner," said Greg. "Is he who you thought he is?"

"I'm still not sure," said Larry.

"Larry, you know what I think?" said Greg. "I think you're just a little bit off your rocker."

"Thanks," replied Larry. "I was beginning to think that I'm *way* off my rocker."

There was a strange car parked in the driveway in front of his father's office when Larry got home, indicating that his father was busy with a client.

He walked into the house, expecting his mother to be in the kitchen, the dining room, the living room, or somewhere else in the house. She wasn't.

He returned to the living room, took off his cleats and slumped into an easy chair. He was exhausted, thirsty and hungry. He wished that he had accepted the man's offer of a Coke or an ice-cream cone. As a matter of fact, he almost had; just having heard the man mention those tasty items had whetted his appetite.

Not until a sharp voice had brought him bolt upright did he realize that he had dozed off.

"Larry! Wake up!"

He opened his eyes, stared at his mother. "Wow!" he said. "I was really asleep, wasn't I?"

"You sure were. And you should know better than to sit in that chair in that dirty uniform," she admonished him. "Son, I just don't know what I'm going to do with you."

"You don't have to do *anything* with me, Mom," he said, getting off the chair and picking up his cleats. A lump rose in his throat as he started to go by her.

Suddenly she reached out and grabbed his arm. He looked at her, and saw a smile come over her face. Her eyes warmed.

"Hey, I'm sorry I yelled. You must have come home just after I left," she said quietly. "I went over to Helen's to borrow some coffee. I was only gone about ten minutes."

"I guess I was tired," he said.

"Okay. Get out of that messy uniform and wash up, while I get your supper ready. You must be starved."

He smiled, realizing that he felt much less tired now.

Between that night and Saturday afternoon, he thought a great deal about the man who he was ninety-nine percent sure was Yancey Foote.

On Saturday afternoon he walked uptown, taking the same street he and Greg had taken on the day they had followed the man. He came to Berry Avenue, the street on which the man had surprised them, and debated whether to take it or not. He finally decided he would, and walked the length of the block, all the time realizing that it wasn't necessarily on this block that the big guy lived. It could be on the next one, or some other block, for that matter.

After walking a couple of blocks Larry returned to the main street and continued uptown. He reached the heart of the village, turned left on State Street, walked a block, then headed back for home. He was disappointed; he had hoped to meet the man somewhere on the street.

Sure, he was expecting a lot. But a small miracle like that happened sometime, didn't it?

It did happen a short while later.

He was passing by Harry's Grocery Store when its door opened and a voice said, "Hi, Larry! How're you doing?"

Larry stopped short. It was the man he was looking for!

64

"Why, hi, sir," he said, staring surprisedly at him. "I — I'm fine."

"Just a minute," said the man. "I'll pay for my groceries and be right out."

How do you like that? It *was* a miracle!

A few moments later the man came back out, carrying a sack of groceries.

"How about some popcorn while we watch a football game on TV?" he asked, smiling broadly. "I just live around the corner."

Larry's mouth was ajar, but the words just wouldn't come.

"I saw you walk by a little while ago," the man continued, towering in front of Larry. "You were heading uptown."

"I — I was looking for you," Larry confessed.

The man grinned. "I sort of figured you were," he said.

The door of the grocery store opened and Harry, the fat old man who owned the store, popped his head out. "Mr. Lacey," he said, "you forgot your magazine."

He brought it to the man, and Larry recognized

65

it instantly. It was a copy of the same magazine he had purchased. The magazine with the article about Yancey Foote in it.

"Oh, thanks, Harry," said Mr. Lacey. *Mr. Lacey? Was that his name?* "You're a gentleman," he added.

"You paid for it," replied Harry. Smiling, he went back into the store.

Twin suns reflected on Mr. Lacey's glasses. "Come on," he said. "We'll watch a football game and pop some corn. You can call your Mom or Dad from my apartment and tell them you're there. Okay?"

"Okay," Larry said, forgetting everything he had ever been told about being wary of strangers.

"Fine. Come on."

They walked up the street, turned left at the corner and turned in at the third house. They entered by the front door just as a plump, middle-aged woman came down a flight of stairs, carrying a vacuum cleaner and a feather duster.

"Oh, hi, Mr. Lacey," she greeted him pleasantly. "I just cleaned your room. Not that it really

66

needed it, but dust does have a habit of collecting, you know."

Mr. Lacey smiled. "Yes, I know, Mrs. Franklin. Thank you. By the way, this young friend of mine is Larry Shope, star football player for the Digits."

"I'm pleased to meet you, Larry," she said, extending a thin, frail-looking hand.

"I'm pleased to meet you, too," replied Larry, taking her hand.

Then they climbed the stairs to the second floor where Mr. Lacey unlocked a door, went in and put the sack of groceries on a table.

"The phone's there by the sofa," he said. "Why don't you call your parents now?"

Larry did. He let the phone ring ten times, but no one answered.

"No one's home," he said, hanging up the phone.

"Well, try later on," Mr. Lacey suggested. "Have a chair."

Mr. Lacey went to a console television set and turned it on, while Larry sat down on a wide, yellow sofa, facing it. On the set was a silver cup, the size of a short drinking glass, with a football on it.

"Make yourself at home," said Mr. Lacey. "I'll get the corn popping."

A football game was being televised, but what captured Larry's interest was the football on the television set. There was something written on it in white ink.

As he began hearing and smelling the corn popping in the kitchen, he got up and went to the television set. Plain as could be the inscription on the football read:

Winning ball. Touchdown scored against Baltimore Colts by Yancey Foote.

A WAVE OF apprehension rolled over Larry. He felt a chill, as if the temperature in the room had suddenly dropped. Feeling as if he had invaded a man's privacy, he started to turn and saw Mr. Lacey — *why did you change your name, Yancey?* — standing in the doorway, looking at him.

Larry blushed. "I'd better go," he said, struggling to get the words out.

Yancey Foote smiled. "Why? Because you found out I'm really Yancey Foote? Don't be silly. Sit down. Take the load off your feet. Why do you think I invited you here, anyway?"

Larry's skin prickled. "I *knew* you were Yancey Foote. I just knew it. But why are you going by the name of Mr. Lacey?"

Yancey took off his sunglasses and Larry stared at his eyes. They were *definitely* Yancey Foote's!

"I've only told a couple of people — Mrs. Franklin and Harry the grocer," he answered. "I suppose it might not have made a bit of difference if I had really told everyone the truth. But I thought that, for a while at least, I'd keep my secret."

"Why?" Larry asked curiously. "Are you really in bad trouble, Yancey? I mean, Mr. Foote?"

"Yancey's all right," said Yancey. "After all, that's how you were addressing your letters to me. Right?"

"Right." Larry shook his head. "Boy, was I worried when I didn't hear from you anymore!"

"I'm sure sorry about that," Yancey said contritely. "But lately I haven't had time to answer any of the fans."

They both seemed to realize at the same time that the corn popping machine had stopped.

"Take a seat," said Yancey. "I'll be right back."

He was back in a minute with two large bowls of popcorn, one of which he handed to Larry. Then he sat down on the sofa, and while munching on the popcorn, explained why he had not answered Larry's letters.

"It started with a stupid argument in a barroom," he said. "A couple of my friends would usually go with me, but this time I went alone. We were playing cards in my room and I went out to get something to eat and drink. I had given the bartender my order and was waiting for him to bring it when a guy comes up to me and starts rattling off about how much better the Packers would be if I played with somebody else. I grinned at him and told him that he could be right, but that I had no intention of encouraging them to make that decision. He kept needling me, then gave me a shove and called me a couple of unpleasant names."

"Is that when you hit him?"

"No. I pushed him back first, and he went out the door, grumbling. A few minutes later I paid for my drink and left. That's when he jumped me. Just outside the door. Came at me with a bottle."

"The stinker," said Larry.

"He was worse than a stinker. But it was either him or me."

"Wasn't that self-defense?"

"Yes, but there were no witnesses," answered Yancey. "Even inside the building there were only two guys and the bartender. All of them were too interested in watching TV to see what was going on between us."

Yancey paused and popped a few popcorns into his mouth while he glanced at the television set. A college football game was on, but Larry had no interest in watching it. Not at the moment, anyway. Nothing could hold his interest more now than the man sitting beside him and the sad, true tale he had just told.

Yancey crunched on a mouthful of popcorn before he went on. "So, another reason why I came here. When you first wrote you said your dad was a lawyer, and I realized he must be the famous Mr. Shope. When I got in trouble I thought that maybe your dad might help me. Even though you had seldom written about him I had hopes of his being willing to defend me. Because I need a good lawyer to help me out of this mess, big fella."

Larry's heart pounded. When he didn't answer immediately Yancey looked at him. "What's the matter? Why so quiet all of a sudden?"

"Yancey, my father only knows about the first letter," Larry confessed, a lump rising in his throat. "He hardly ever seems interested in football, so I didn't tell him about the others. I don't think our friendship will make him defend you."

"I see," said Yancey. He paused, as if somewhat surprised. "Does he like football? Does he ever watch it on television?"

"Very seldom."

"Well, don't blame him for that," replied Yancey, tossing a couple of popcorns into his mouth. "He's a busy man. Anyway, there are plenty of fans around to keep the sport alive. Right?"

"Right."

Talking about his father reminded Larry of how

rarely he and his father saw each other. His heart ached just thinking about it. Not even the letters he had written to and received from Yancey had ever helped to fill that gap.

At last he finished his popcorn. He put the bowl aside and stood up.

"I think I'd better go, Yancey," he said. "Thanks for the popcorn."

"That's all right," Yancey said, rising. "But wait a minute. I've got something I want you to take back with you. A couple of football plays."

Larry's eyes widened. Football plays?

Yancey went to a desk, pulled out a drawer and took out a long, white envelope.

"Here," he said, handing them to Larry. "Give them to your coach. They're not hard to pull off, but they're pretty effective. Of course I don't expect you guys to run them like we do. But, after a few practices, you should do a good job with them. I've watched your games and none of your plays seem to have much strategy. That's okay when you first start playing. But with your expe-

rience you should be able to pull off some razzle-dazzle stuff."

Larry beamed. "Is that what these plays are? Razzle-dazzle?"

"Well — something like that," Yancey said, grinning.

They shook hands.

"You want me to talk to my father about your wanting to see him?" Larry asked. "Or are you going to call him yourself?"

"I'll call him," said Yancey, walking to the door with Larry. "Thanks for coming over, Larry. I'll see you again soon. Right?"

"Right. And thanks for asking me over, Yancey. I guess, well — I'm *sure* it's one of the nicest afternoons I've ever spent in my life."

"Nice of you to say that, Larry," Yancey replied. "Take care, now."

Larry left the house and headed for Main Street, looking back twice before he reached the intersection. He felt as if he had just stepped out of a dream. Who would ever believe that he had

76

just spent an afternoon with Yancey Foote, the Green Bay Packers' outstanding guard? Nobody.

Except, maybe, Greg Moore.

"He'd be the only guy I'd tell it to, anyway," said Larry, smiling proudly to himself.

9

THE HOUSE WAS locked when Larry got home. He found the key that was kept in a secret hiding place, unlocked the door and went in.

Where were his mother and father? They hadn't told him that they'd be leaving the house.

He saw a note on the table, and picked it up.

> *Dear Larry,* he read,
>
> *Your father and I are driving to the shopping plaza to look for a new rug for the living room.*
>
> *We should be home by 3.*
>
> *Love,*
Mother

He glanced at the clock on the kitchen counter. Three fifteen. Looking for a new rug was taking them longer than his mother had expected.

He went to his room and removed the play patterns from the envelope. The first one was a running play which Yancey had marked *Mash 41*. The second was a pass play he had marked *Swing Pass*. Neither was similar to any of the plays Coach Ellis had taught the Digits.

Larry was still studying them when he heard a car driving in. He soon left his room, leaving the play patterns on the counter above which he kept a stack of books, knickknacks and miniature statues of presidents.

"Hi, Mom," he greeted his mother, meeting her in the anteroom off the kitchen where she was hanging up her coat. "Did you get a rug?"

"Yes!" she answered, her face and eyes beaming, showing her happiness. "It's beige and it's just beautiful. You'll love it, Larry."

Mr. Shope entered a few moments later, flashing a smile that matched his wife's enthusiasm.

"Well, hi, Son," he greeted Larry amiably. "When did you get home?"

"At three fifteen," Larry answered.

"You just walked uptown and back?" his father asked, pulling off his coat. "It seemed that you would've been back before we'd left."

"I met somebody," said Larry.

"Oh? Who?"

Larry hesitated. "A guy named Yancey Foote," he answered at last, wondering if his father would remember the name.

Mr. Shope paused in the act of hanging up his coat, turned and frowned at him. "Yancey Foote? The same Yancey Foote who played guard with the Green Bay Packers? The guy you wrote to?"

Surprised, Larry stared at him. "Yes! Then you *do* remember!" he cried happily.

"Of course, I do. I've also read that he had gotten into some kind of trouble," his father went on, hanging up the coat. When he gazed back at Larry again he was smiling. "Now just where did you meet this Yancey Foote and what did you two football players talk about, anyway?"

"He's teasing me," Larry thought. "He thinks I was daydreaming."

"On Main Street," Larry said seriously. "He was coming out of a grocery store."

"And you knew it was he right away — just like that," his father said, snapping his fingers.

Larry shook his head. "No. I wasn't absolutely sure then. He was wearing a beard and dark sunglasses. It wasn't till later, at his apartment, that I found out for sure."

His father's brows knitted. "At his apartment?"

"Yes. I tried to call you and Mom on the phone, but you weren't home. I've been a great fan of his, Dad. I've been writing to him almost a couple of years now, and he's answered every one of my letters except the last two."

Mr. Shope took Larry's arm, led him into the living room and sat down. It was clear now, by the expression on his face, that he had taken an interest in his son's story.

"I remember sometime ago your telling me that you had written to him, Larry," he admitted. "But you had never told me that you'd written more than once."

"I know. I — I didn't think you were interested," answered Larry, his voice shaky.

"I see." Mr. Shope paused, and seemed to be reflecting on Larry's words. "You said that you had found out for sure that he's Yancey Foote. How did you find out?"

"There was a football on the TV set with his name on it," Larry replied. "He also told me about himself and the trouble he had gotten into. Besides, he gave me two play patterns for our team to use."

His father remained silent for a long minute, as if baffled by this close, unusual friendship between his son and a famous football player.

"I can hardly believe it, Son," he said at last. "It seems to me that Yancey has confided in you an awful lot. If you were a grown-up, someone he knew very well — "

"But he does know me well, Dad," Larry inter-

rupted seriously. "I had told him a lot about me and our family, too. That's one of the reasons he came here to Glen Rose."

His father frowned. "What do you mean?"

"He wants you to be his lawyer. He's going to call you up and ask you. I hope you'll help him, Dad. He's really a great guy."

His father kept staring at him, not saying a word for a long time.

Larry showed the play patterns to Coach Ellis on Monday, explaining that a friend of his had drawn them up for him. The team practiced the plays, but concentrated mainly on *Mash 41*, which Coach Ellis promised to try in the game against the Crickets on Tuesday.

Game time finally approached. It was not until the second quarter, though, with the Crickets leading 7–0 and pushing the Digits against their own end zone, when Joe Racino came racing in, replacing Jim Collins at guard.

"Mash forty-one!" he said in the huddle. "The coach says that now's the time."

"I'll say it is," snorted Doug Shaffer, and pinned his eyes on Larry and George Daley. "And I hope that *you* guys remember what to do!"

Unflinching, Larry returned the grim look. "It's your job to pull off that fake run, Doug," he said, trying to keep his cool.

"Don't worry about me," replied Doug.

"Okay. On three," said George.

They broke out of the huddle and ran to the line of scrimmage. The ball was on their own eighteen. It was second and ten. Larry got over the ball, clamped his hands around it.

"Six! Eight! Hut one! Hut two! Hut three!"

Larry snapped the ball.

George took it, hugged it to him, turned, handed it off to Manny Anderson, then faked a pitchout to Doug. Doug rushed around Billy James and right end Ray Bridges, his arms crossed over his chest as if he had the ball.

Manny, who had the ball, bolted through the number one hole, getting excellent blocking as he sped across the twenty . . . the twenty-five . . . the thirty . . . the thirty-five . . .

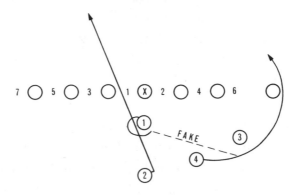

"Go, Manny, go!" Larry yelled as he saw the halfback tearing toward the sideline.

Manny crossed the fifty-yard line and was on the Crickets' thirty-two when their safety man finally reached him and pulled him down. A fifty-four yard run!

"Not bad," said George, grinning happily in the huddle. "Let's give it to them again. They'll never expect that play twice in a row."

"Won't work," countered Doug. "Let me try a crossbuck."

"Come on, Doug," Larry protested. "Let him call it."

"But it's like expecting lightning to strike twice in the same spot," argued Doug.

"Name it, George," said Larry, ignoring him.

"I did," the quarterback replied. "Mash forty-one."

Larry glanced grimly at Doug. "You've got to pull off that fake like you did the first time, Doug, or it surely won't work."

"I'll do my job," Doug grumbled. "You do yours."

The play worked perfectly, Manny having almost an easier time of it than before. Doug's kick for the extra point was good. 7–7.

A few moments later the whistle shrilled, ending the first half. As the teams ran off the field and headed for the locker rooms, Larry glanced toward the sideline. As he expected, he easily spotted Yancey.

Larry waved to him and Yancey smiled, raising two fingers in a V.

Larry remembered that Yancey had not yet called his father.

Had he changed his mind? Did he plan on getting another lawyer? Just what were his plans?

Well, only time would tell.

10.

THE CRICKETS SCORED their second touchdown within the first three minutes of the third quarter. Muggsy Shaw, their husky fullback, went over on a twenty-six-yard run, then booted the ball between the uprights for the extra point. Crickets 14, Digits 7.

The teams lined up for the kickoff. Muggsy, booting for the Crickets, laid one end over end to the thirty-five-yard line, where Billy James caught it and ran it back up the field, dodging three would-be tacklers before being pulled down on the forty-four.

"Twenty-six," said George in the huddle.

Billy James took the pitchout from George and bolted through the six hole for three yards.

"Let's try an end-around this time," said George. "Their weak side seems to be on the left. You ready for another shot at it, Billy?"

"Weak side on the left?" Doug echoed. "Neither side looks weak to me."

"Well, it *is* a little weaker," George said, as if determined not to let Doug change his mind. "Let's go. On three!"

Larry snapped the ball and charged forward, his target the Crickets' middle linebacker, Jim Green. Jim was tall, strong and fast. Just the sight of his speed triggered a wave of fear in Larry. "Look at the way he lifts his knees," Larry thought. "If I throw him a block they could easily hit me on the chin and probably knock me out."

He erased the frightening thought, realizing that it might slow him up in his drive to block Jim. He was still chasing the linebacker, was only inches away from him, when Jim threw himself at Billy and flattened him out like a pancake.

A loss of two yards.

90

"Well, who was right?" Doug's puffed-up ego showed in his smile. The two-yard loss seemed unimportant to him.

"Okay, you were," George admitted. "But — "

"It was my fault," Larry broke in. "If I had blocked Jim as I should have, he'd never have gotten Billy."

"You want to know the truth, Larry?" said Doug. "You couldn't have blocked him if you were Larry Csonka."

"Let's play ball," Greg's voice cut in sharply. "We're wasting time."

Third and nine.

"Now's the time for the Swing Pass, the other play Yancey Foote gave us," Larry thought.

"Flair pass," said George.

On the snap he faded back, while both ends ran down the field, and heaved a long one to Curt down the left side. It was too long, sailing over Curt's head for an incompleted pass.

"How about trying the Swing Pass?" Larry said in the huddle.

"Why not?" said George, ignoring the fact that

it was fourth down. "Curt, Manny, Doug — you know what to do. Let's go! Swing Pass! On two!"

SWING PASS

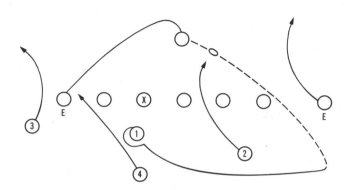

On the snap George faded back, Curt started off slowly in a diagonal run up the field, Manny circled in toward the line of scrimmage then cut out toward the left sideline, Doug faked taking a pitchout from George and bolted toward the three hole, and Billy ran in toward the center of the field. Suddenly Curt stopped, then cut back a couple of steps just as George heaved the pass.

On target!

Curt, with five yards between him and the nearest Cricket, had clear sailing in front of him and went for a touchdown.

"It worked!" Greg shouted, pounding Larry enthusiastically on the back. "It worked!"

"I never had any doubt about it," answered Larry, restraining a smile. In a moment, though, his face lit up brightly, as he glanced toward the sideline where he had seen Yancey earlier. The big man seemed to catch his glance for he raised two fingers again in a V sign.

"Have you met him yet?" Greg asked.

Larry nodded. "Last Saturday."

"Really?"

"Really."

Doug kicked for the point after, but missed.

"Nuts!" he snorted.

Boots Johnson, the Crickets' running back who played in the right corner facing the Digits, caught Doug's kick and ran it back to his thirty-nine. Muggsy Shaw plowed through the line twice for a total gain of eight yards, then was stopped cold on the line of scrimmage as he tried to make it three gains in a row.

Fourth and two. The Crickets went into a punt formation, and Muggsy again was the focus of attention as he booted the ball to the Digits' thirty-six-yard line.

Doug smashed through for an eleven-yard gain on the first play, then picked up only two on the next.

They tried *Mash 41* again for a fifteen-yard gain, then a second time in hopes for a repetition. Instead, Manny, as he reached for the ball from George, lost control of it. And, during the scramble that followed, he lost possession of it, too.

"My fault," Manny apologized solemnly.

"Forget it," said George. "Maybe we're working that play too much. They're bound to catch on after a while."

"I think they have," Doug said.

The Crickets moved the ball, getting it to the Digits' forty-one when the buzzer sounded, ending the third quarter.

The teams exchanged sides. The Crickets kept moving, gains being shared by Muggsy Shaw, Boots Johnson and Bob Blair, their other running back. They were chewing up yardage slowly: three . . . one . . . six . . . eight . . .

"What I'd do to bust their fat balloon," Larry said to Greg as they waited for the Crickets to file to the line of scrimmage for the umpteenth time.

Greg shrugged. "Make 'em fumble," he said. "Or tackle 'em before they gain a yard. The answer's easy, if you could do it."

Larry grimaced. "Ask a stupid question . . ."

"Right," Greg said, grinning.

The Crickets advanced the ball to the Digits' nine-yard line. There were less than two minutes left to play.

"Watch for a pass," Doug warned.

They watched, and it came. Larry sensed it even before Todd threw the ball. He could tell by Todd's actions where the target was, too. He sprinted to his right.

The ball came spiraling through the air. Larry leaped, caught it, brought it down to his chest and

started to bolt up the field. He eluded a linebacker, got blocking on another, and raced all the way. He ran harder and harder, never looking back, never hearing the cries that began to rise from the Digits' fans, never hearing anything until he had crossed the goal line.

Seconds later Doug kicked for the point after. This time it was good. Digits 20, Crickets 14.

"That was another way," Greg said, cracking a broad smile.

11

LARRY, WALKING HOME with Greg and
Yancey Foote, was aware of a following close
behind them: Doug, Billy, Ray and Paul.

"This is my friend, Greg Moore," Larry said to
Yancey. "He's quite deaf. You have to look at him
when you speak to him."

"Hi, Greg," Yancey said, shaking Greg's hand.
"You played a nice game."

"Thanks, sir. That last play Larry made was
just great, wasn't it, Mr. Foote?"

"Sure was. And it came at the right time, too,"
said Yancey.

Larry wondered if Yancey had telephoned his father yet, but didn't think that this was the proper time to ask him. It would embarrass Yancey. And those big ears behind them might just relish every word of it, too.

After Greg left and the four guys moved off in their respective directions, Yancey continued walking with Larry.

"Now that those guys are out of earshot," he said, "I can talk to you. Did you tell your father about me? I intend to call him this evening."

"I told him," Larry answered.

"What did he say?"

"The moment I mentioned your name he knew what team you played on and about the trouble you're in."

"Goes to show that he reads the sports pages," said Yancey. "Did you tell him that I'd like to have him as my lawyer?"

"Yes."

"What did he say to that?"

"He didn't."

99

Yancey frowned. "He didn't say he would, or wouldn't?"

"That's right. He didn't say one way or the other. I guess you'll have to see him about that."

They walked on silently for a while, still heading toward Larry's home which was about a half a block away now.

"Think he's home?" Yancey asked. "I might as well see him now if I can, or make an appointment with him if he's busy."

"If he's not downtown or with a client, he'll see you," Larry said.

The family car was the only one in the driveway when they arrived at the house, a good sign that his father was alone.

He was.

"Dad, this is Yancey Foote," Larry introduced the football star to his father, who stared at Yancey as if he had just met Hercules himself. "He'd like to talk to you."

They shook hands.

"Pleased to meet you, Mr. Shope," said Yancey.

"Same here, Mr. Foote," said Mr. Shope. "Larry's told me about you. I understand you've become pretty close friends."

"That's right. You have a nice son. I bet you're very proud of him."

Mr. Shope smiled at Larry. "I am. I'm very proud of him," he said.

Larry met his eyes, then looked away. "Are you really proud of me, Dad?" he thought. "Why? Because I don't ask you to play football catch with me? Because I don't ask you to take me to baseball games, and hockey games, and play Chinese checkers in between times? Oh, sure, Dad. You must be very proud of me that I don't interrupt you from spending so much time with your great law practice."

"Come in and sit down, Mr. Foote," Mr. Shope invited genially. "Larry, I — " He hesitated.

"This business is between you and Yancey, Dad," Larry interrupted. "Anyway, I've got to get out of these duds and wash up."

He left, closing the office door softly behind

him, and smiled. "Dad will defend Yancey and win the case, too," he thought. "He's really a great guy. He really is."

Within a week progress had been made in the case, *People vs. Yancey Foote*. With the cooperation of Judge Irma Standish a jury was selected and trial set for October 24, a Friday.

"You think he has a good chance, Dad?" Larry asked anxiously at the supper table as the day of the trial drew near.

"I think so," his father replied, stabbing a carrot with his fork. "He was an orphan. Did you know that, Larry? He grew up in an orphanage. He was a big kid and nobody wanted to adopt him. When he reached his teens he got a job, saved money, played high school football and paid his way through college. He didn't play football until his senior year."

"Yes, I know all that, Dad," answered Larry proudly. "He made the Athlete-of-the-Week twice that year, then was the Packers' number three draft choice."

"Hey, man, I guess you do know about him!" His father smiled.

"Very interesting," smiled Mrs. Shope. "But a man his size *has* to play pro football to earn the fortune he needs to feed himself. Larry, pass me the salt and pepper, please."

On Tuesday the Digits discovered that the Finbacks were not really the threat they were feared to be. At least, they didn't show it in the first quarter. The Finbacks had whipped Moon City and the Moths by marginal scores, but had lost to the Crickets.

The second quarter got under way with the Digits leading 13–0, a comfortable lead. The score remained that way till the middle of the third quarter when Manny caught a twenty-two-yard pass on the Finbacks' forty-one, and went all the way for his second touchdown of the game. Doug tried the point-after kick, but failed for the second time to boot the pigskin between the uprights. 19–0, Digits.

"Well, it's a good thing we're ahead of them,"

Doug said sourly. "Maybe you'd better let somebody else kick for the extra point next time, George."

"What a switch," thought Larry. He had never heard Doug pitying himself before.

Doug was still tops in the kickoff department, however. The ball sailed end over end into Finbacks territory, landing in left halfback Dutch Pawling's arms. Larry was among the crowd that went after him, feeling confident that Dutch would be lucky to get within fifteen yards of midfield.

Dutch did better than that. Besides getting excellent blocking, he did some fancy hip-swiveling, too, twice wiggling himself free of Digits' clutches. Then, for the last twenty-six yards, he had clear sailing and went for a touchdown.

"I can't believe it!" exclaimed George, pounding his helmet with his fists.

"You'd better believe it," Larry said.

Fullback Paul Henley made the point-after kick good. Digits 19, Finbacks 7.

In the fourth quarter the Finbacks picked up

seven more points. Not easily, though. They had to punt twice to get the ball deep into Digits territory. But it was the punts that helped, and then Dutch's crossbuck run that put him just across the goal line.

Again Paul's kick was good. But the Finbacks couldn't keep up the fire, and the game went to the Digits, 19–14.

"Man, am I glad that's over," said Greg, walking off the field with Larry, helmet in his hand, sweat pouring from his face. "Those guys were coming up fast."

"Telling me," said Larry.

Yancey was waiting for them at the gate. The broad smile on his face gave no hint that his court trial was pending.

"Well, guys, you pulled those plays off like pros," he said proudly.

Larry smiled. "You drew them up so well, Yancey," he said, "that we *couldn't* miss."

"Got any new ones for us, Yancey?" Greg asked.

"Frankly, Greg, I haven't given it a thought;

had other things on my mind. I'll try to have another one for you by Monday, though. Okay?"

"You don't have to, Yancey," Larry replied. "We know you're pretty busy."

Not even a pro football star, he reflected, should be thinking about play patterns when his own trial is coming up.

"That's okay," Yancey insisted. "I'll have a play for you. Maybe a couple of them."

12

THE TRIAL LASTED two days, Friday and Monday. It was almost five o'clock on Monday when the case went to the jury.

By the next afternoon the jury was still deliberating.

"What rotten luck," Larry said to Greg as they headed for the field to play their final game of the season, against the Moths. "I was hoping that the jury would have their verdict by this morning, anyway."

"My parents said that sometimes a jury could be working on a case for days," said Greg.

"That's right," agreed Larry, who had learned a little about law from his father.

The day was cold in spite of the sun popping out from behind white clouds now and then. The crowd was the largest that had attended any of the Digits' games this season. Maybe the Digits' spreading reputation as a winning team was responsible. A winning team always drew the fans. And the Digits, having won their last two games, was certainly a winning team.

"Oh, well," thought Larry, "who cares how many fans are here? I just hope that Yancey is found not guilty. As a matter of fact, I would rather lose the game than have him be found guilty."

During the game he felt scared each time the Moths had the ball. He wondered whether he'd ever get over the feeling when meeting a runner head-on, or throwing himself at a ball carrier, or throwing a block on a guy. "How long will I have to play before that scared feeling wears off, anyway?" he asked himself.

It wasn't till the end of the first three minutes

of the second quarter when Sammy Shantz, the Moths' safety man, intercepted one of George Daley's long passes and ran sixty-three yards; the first score of the game went up on the scoreboard. Franky Milo kicked for the point after and made it good. 7–0.

Two minutes later, with the ball back in the Moths' possession on their own forty-two, Sammy Shantz's pitchout to Earl Dimmick, his left halfback, was fumbled, and Larry was one of the first to go busting through the line in a wild scramble to recover it. He saw the ball popping like a cork out of one and then another guy's hands, and finally saw it rolling freely across the grass turf. Out of the corner of his eye he saw Franky making a mad dash for it. At the same time Larry bolted after it, too, and got to it a fraction of a second before Franky did. He pulled it under him and lay on it, while Franky tried vainly to take it from him.

The whistle shrilled. Digits' ball.

"Mash forty-one," George said in the huddle.

The play worked for twenty-eight yards. An

end-around run by Doug Shaffer accounted for sixteen more. They were on the go now, with short runs, short passes. They were moving . . . moving . . .

They got to the Moths' two, and Doug went over for the touchdown. He kicked successfully for the extra point, too. 7–7.

Minutes later the whistle announcing the end of the half came as a surprise. The time had really zipped by.

Coach Ellis's talk during the intermission was filled with its usual "go-get-'em-guys-you've-got-it-in-you" spirit. But only some of it filtered through Larry's busy mind. He was wondering how the jury was doing on Yancey Foote's case.

Franky Milo, after two short runs, took a pitch-out from Sammy, then faded back and winged a long pass to his right end, Peter Buttrick. Peter went all the way to the Digits' three-yard line, where George pulled him down. Then Sammy went over on a quarterback sneak for the Moths' second touchdown. Again Franky's kick was good. Moths 14, Digits 7.

The Moths kept pressing, forcing the Digits back against their own end zone again, and Larry wondered what the Digits fans thought of them now. The Digits certainly were not the same fighting, spirited team that had defeated the Crickets and the Finbacks. What had happened to that fighting spirit, anyway?

With fourth down and the ball on their eight-yard line, Larry thought of one of the two plays that Yancey had given him last Sunday.

"How about trying the Fake Punt, George?" he said. "This might be a good time for it."

George looked at him. "One of those new plays? I don't know. We could be tackled back here and give them a safety."

"Or we could pull the biggest fake of the year," said Larry.

"Okay, let's try it," said George.

The team went into a punt formation. George called signals. Larry snapped the ball.

George took the long spiraling snap from Larry, started to kneel with it, then got up and sprinted

112

toward the right side of the line. With fine blocking from Billy, Doug and Ray, he churned up
yardage till he reached the Moths' thirty-eight.

FAKE PUNT
K–1 Right

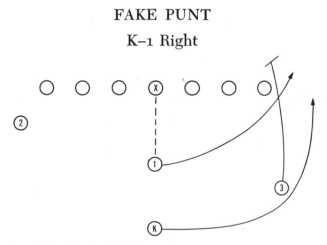

"We did it!" cried Larry happily.

From there the Moths slowed the Digits' forward progress, but the Digits managed to get to
the Moths' eighteen, where they were held for
three downs without gaining a yard.

"Doug, think you can boot one over?" asked
George.

"Why not?" replied Doug. "I can't miss *all* the time."

He kicked, and it was good. The field goal made the score 14–10, the Moths still leading.

The score remained unchanged to the middle of the fourth quarter. The Moths had possession of the ball on the Digits' nine when Franky dropped a pitchout. Larry, plowing through like a wild buffalo, picked up the ball, carried it for eight yards and was dropped like a sack of potatoes.

"Nice going, Larry!" Greg exclaimed, slapping him on the back.

On two plays they gained four yards. The situation looked glum.

"Swing Pass," said George.

The play worked for twenty-one yards.

They tried it again. It went incomplete. Again they tried it, and again it went incomplete.

Third down and ten, on their forty-two.

"How much time left?" George asked the referee.

"Fifty seconds," answered the official.

114

The guys stared at each other, eyes like black holes, faces smeared with dirt and sweat.

"Four Shotgun," said George. "And it better work."

Larry's heart beat fast. *Four Shotgun* was the other play that Yancey had given him last Sunday. It called for the quarterback to stay in his regular position behind the center, and the other backfield men to line up behind the right tackle. If it worked, Doug, taking the pitchout from George, could gain substantial yardage.

FOUR SHOTGUN

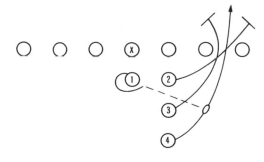

They broke out of the huddle and rushed to the scrimmage line.

"Forty-six! Thirteen! Hut! Hut! Hut!"

Larry snapped the ball. George took it, spun around to his left, then pitched the ball out to Doug as he started to run behind Billy James. The fullback bolted through the hole that yawned before him like a tunnel, legs churning like pistons as they gulped up yardage. Sammy brought him down on the Moths' fourteen.

"Thirty-eight seconds," informed the ref.

"Let's try it again," said Larry anxiously.

"Why not?" exclaimed Doug, his face glistening with sweat.

They did. This time Doug carried it to the twelve-yard line, where he was smeared.

"Twelve yards from home," said George in the huddle. "Let's try the keeper. Larry, Greg — everybody — I'm depending on you."

They did the job, opening up a hole wide enough for George to barrel through. Touchdown!

Doug kicked for the extra point, and it was good. 14–17, Digits.

Seconds later the game ended, the Digits jumping and cheering with the sweet taste of victory.

As Larry sprinted past the bleachers in his eagerness to get home, he heard a voice yelling to him, "Larry, wait!"

He stopped, and stared. It was his father!

"Dad!"

Next to his father stood Yancey! Both of them were smiling! He ran to them, took their extended hands.

"Nice game, Son!" exclaimed Mr. Shope. "I'm sure glad I didn't miss this one!"

"It was a great finish, Larry," said Yancey, his face beaming.

"I know how *we* came out!" Larry cried. "It's how *you* came out, Yancey, that I'm anxious to know about!"

"Oh. We won, too," Yancey said, his eyes flashing. "Your father's one of the best doggone lawyers that has ever come down the pike. Do you know that, Larry?"

Larry's eyes danced. "I've *always* known that, Yancey," he said.

Mr. Shope, holding Larry's hand, squeezed it warmly.

"From now on I'm going to see to it that that word *lawyers* is interchangeable with *fathers*," he vowed. "Shall we go? Your mother promised to cook us a big dinner — win or lose."

How many of these Matt Christopher sports classics have you read?

- ❑ Baseball Pals
- ❑ The Basket Counts
- ❑ Catch That Pass!
- ❑ Catcher with a Glass Arm
- ❑ Challenge at Second Base
- ❑ The Counterfeit Tackle
- ❑ The Diamond Champs
- ❑ Dirt Bike Racer
- ❑ Dirt Bike Runaway
- ❑ Face-Off
- ❑ Football Fugitive
- ❑ The Fox Steals Home
- ❑ The Great Quarterback Switch
- ❑ Hard Drive to Short
- ❑ The Hockey Machine
- ❑ Ice Magic
- ❑ Johnny Long Legs
- ❑ The Kid Who Only Hit Homers
- ❑ Little Lefty
- ❑ Long Shot for Paul
- ❑ Long Stretch at First Base
- ❑ Look Who's Playing First Base
- ❑ Miracle at the Plate
- ❑ No Arm in Left Field
- ❑ Red-Hot Hightops
- ❑ Run, Billy, Run
- ❑ Shortstop from Tokyo
- ❑ Soccer Halfback
- ❑ The Submarine Pitch
- ❑ Tackle Without a Team
- ❑ Tight End
- ❑ Too Hot to Handle
- ❑ Touchdown for Tommy
- ❑ Tough to Tackle
- ❑ Wingman on Ice
- ❑ The Year Mom Won the Pennant

All available in paperback from Little, Brown and Company

Join the Matt Christopher Fan Club!

To become an official member of the Matt Christopher Fan Club,
send a self-addressed, stamped envelope (10 x 13, 3 oz. of postage) to:

Matt Christopher Fan Club
34 Beacon Street
Boston, MA 02108